Buck Wilder's Adventures

Book #5

THE SALMON STOP RUNNING

Buck Wilder

Other Buck Wilder Books

Buck Wilder's Adventures
#1 Who Stole the Animal Poop?
#2 The Work Bees Go on Strike
#3 The Ants Dig to China
#4 The Owls Don't Give a Hoot
#6 The Squirrels Go Nuts

Buck Wilder's Animal Wisdom
Buck Wilder's Small Fry Fishing Guide
Buck Wilder's Small Twig Hiking and Camping Guide
Buck Wilder's Little Skipper Boating Guide

...and more to come...

Buck Wilder's Animal Adventures #5: The Salmon Stop Running
Written by Timothy R. Smith

First Edition
Library of Congress Cataloging-in-Publication Data

Smith, Timothy R.

Buck Wilder's Adventures #5
The Salmon Stop Running

Summary: Who stole our river? That's what the animals of the forest want to
know! Their once free-flowing river is now nothing but a big lake, and the
salmon are stuck swimming around in circles.

ISBN-13: 978-0-9643793-8-1

Fiction
10 9 8 7 6 5 4 3 2

Buck Wilder's Adventures
4160 M-72 East
Williamsburg, MI 49690

www.buckwilder.com

Buck Wilder

"Don't fool with Mother Nature."
B.W.

THE SALMON STOP RUNNING

CHAPTERS

INTRODUCTION

This is where your imagination really counts, in the start of this story, right here in the introduction. Imagine you are in the woods, a really big woods, full of big trees. The crunch of pine needles is under your feet and the smell of earthy moss is in the air. You look up and in front of you is a huge log house that is built up in the tree limbs. It is a big house. It looks quiet, peaceful, and friendly. There are birds in the bird feeders, a few animals sleeping on the porches, and the smell of home cooking coming from the chimney. It looks kind of like this:

As I am sure you already know, inside this big tree house lives the famous Buck Wilder. Outside of the woods not many people know of Buck Wilder, but inside the woods he is very famous. His animal friends just love him. They trust his opinion, like to visit whenever possible, and eat his home cooking. If there is ever a problem in the woods, Buck Wilder is always there to help.

He looks kind of like this:

Buck Wilder's most trusted companion is Rascal Raccoon. Usually, you will find Rascal hanging around Buck's tree house, helping with chores, taking a nap, or feeding the fish in the aquarium. Rascal is an older raccoon, a little larger than normal, with a big appetite and he is a little more mischievous than most. He is a great friend to Buck. By nature he is a good detective and likes to help when a problem or dilemma occurs in the woods.

He looks kind of like this:

Along with Rascal Raccoon, Buck Wilder has many friends that live in the woods surrounding his tree house. They are his animal friends. They visit as much as possible, always hoping for a little of Buck's home cooking and a chance to hear one of Buck's adventure stories. Buck always tells the best stories and the animals love to hear them, because most of the stories are about them. Buck's animal friends look kind of like this:

So, let's read one of Buck Wilder's great adventure stories about the time the salmon stopped running! Turn the page and let's go!

CHAPTER 1

IT ALL STARTED LIKE THIS

One early morning, just before wood-chopping time, Buck Wilder was sitting in his tree house having a morning cup of coffee and writing some notes for his next outdoor adventure story. Buck sometimes likes to write in the morning when his ideas are fresh.

Rascal Raccoon was just having a morning wake-up stretch when all of a sudden the bell went off. It was so loud that even the fish in the aquarium jumped a little. As you know, when the bell goes off it means a visitor has come to see Buck Wilder, and Rascal needs to lower the ladder so that the visitor can climb up into the tree house.

So down came the ladder and up came an old friend, Porcupine Patsy. It had been a long time since Porcupine Patsy had come to the tree house to visit Buck and Rascal. She was in no hurry to climb those steps, but very slowly, one step at a time, she climbed, and with all her long, sharp porcupine quills swinging back and forth, made

it up to the tree house. Porcupine Patsy was an older porcupine who had grown a little chubby in her old age, and had learned that she would eventually get to where she was going, so there was no reason to hurry through life.

As she came into the tree house Buck greeted her with a big and friendly smile. "Welcome Porcupine Patsy. Where have you been? Haven't seen you in a month of Sundays! Come on in and have some breakfast with us. I

21

have some homemade salt crackers and a few leftover pretzels that I think you would just love to chew on." Buck knew that all porcupines, especially Patsy, loved anything with salt on it. He knew porcupines would sometimes go for miles just to take a lick on the side of the road, an old fence post, the side of a picnic table, or anything that might just have a little taste of salt to it.

"Sounds great," said Patsy. "I should come here more often!"

"You sure should," said Buck, "we miss hearing your stories that always get to the point!" At that, everybody gave a little laugh because porcupines have so many quill points on them.

CHAPTER 2

PORCUPINE PATSY NEEDS HELP

"Buck, I didn't come for a social visit, especially so early in the day. I am here for some help and could use your advice."

"Glad to help," said Buck. "What's up?"

"There seems to be a problem in the woods," said Patsy. "And I don't know if it has to do with me or the woods."

"Go ahead. Tell me what is going on," said Buck.

"Well," continued Patsy with a big sigh, "I don't seem to have any friends lately. I am a prickly sort of character and don't move as fast as everybody else. And those that don't know me tend to shy away, but I am likeable and easy going, as you know. I mean no harm to

Whow is me!

anybody. I would only use my sharp quills if there was danger."

"I know that Patsy," replied Buck. "So, again, what's the problem?"

"The problem is," said Patsy sadly, "that all of the animals have left my neighborhood. There is no one left not even a bird flies by. It is as quiet as an empty meadow and I'm getting very lonesome. Everybody is gone."

"Wow," said Buck. "That is serious. I wonder what is going on." Buck sat still for a few minutes scratching his head in deep thought and then said, "Rascal, once again you need to be our detective. Go with Patsy down to the lower end of the woods, that she calls home, look around, check things out, and see if you can find out where all the animals have gone. Look for tracks, sniff around, and let me know what you find out. And here, take these salt crackers and pretzels with you, in case the two of you would like a snack along the way."

"Will do," said Rascal.

Remember to share!

BAG -O- SNACKS

"Thanks a lot," said Patsy. "The next time I come to visit it will be a social call and I'll bring some stories that have a point to them!"

"Hee, hee, hee," giggled Patsy,

as she raised her tail of pointed quills, smiled, and slowly turned to go down the ladder.

CHAPTER 3

WHY WAS IT SO QUIET?

Rascal Raccoon and Porcupine Patsy headed off into the woods toward the neighborhood where Patsy lived. They moved along at a slow and easy pace because that is the way porcupines walk. Rascal understood and politely walked along nice and easy.

Sure enough, as they continued down the trail toward the end of the big woods, Rascal noticed it became

quieter and quieter. It was very unusual because the woods, especially this part of it, was always alive with sounds and music in the air. The sounds came from the water echoing through the woods as it cascaded over falls, pushed against big boulders in the river, and rushed

on down the stream. The music in the woods came from the birds singing, the geese honking, the ducks quacking, and the frogs croaking. But this was different. It was quiet, very quiet. "You are absolutely right," said Rascal to Patsy, as they continued down the trail.

31

"This is almost spooky. I wonder where everyone has gone?" continued Rascal. "Let's go down to the river and find out why we can't hear anything."

"Good idea," said Patsy. "I never thought of that!"

The closer Rascal and Patsy came to the river the more they both realized something was terribly wrong. They couldn't hear of rushing water. When they reached the shore of the river the answer was obvious. The rushing water was gone. It was completely dried up. There was only a small trickle of the stream remaining and it was having a hard time moving downstream against the big boulders and rocks.

CHAPTER 4

WHO STOLE IT?

"Who stole our river?" said Patsy in astonishment. "It's gone! There is hardly anything left of it!"

"I don't know," replied Rascal. "But we had better find out! Things don't look right around here. The plants and flowers along the river bank are all wilted. There are no bees buzzing around them and no butterflies fluttering. Look at the leaves on those nearby trees, they are dried up and the

33

nuts have fallen to the ground. All of the chattering squirrels have gone too. The mud along the edge of the riverbank is drying up and showing big cracks. Look at all the tracks in the dried mud. Turtle tracks, frogs, salamanders, snakes, and geese—everybody has left the water

and headed off into the woods."

"Wow, that is really spooky," said Patsy looking down at the dried-up tracks.

"Most of them seem to be going off this way, heading upstream into the woods," said Rascal as he studied them closer. "Let's follow them and see where they go." So, very slowly and carefully, Rascal and Patsy started heading upstream in the direction of the tracks.

As they slowly moved along the dried-up riverbank they thought they heard sounds coming from up ahead. Sure enough as they moved farther upstream the sounds got louder and clearer. It actually sounded like laughter! "Do you hear what I hear?" asked Rascal.

"Can't be," replied Patsy. "Who could be laughing at a time like this?" But as they moved closer and closer to the noise they realized it was laughter, and lots of it! Ducks were quacking, geese were honking, frogs were croaking, and above it all, you could hear the loud laughing and yelling of the river otters. They were almost screaming with delight!

"What is going on?" said Rascal as he looked ahead in puzzlement.

In front of them stood a huge wall of logs, branches, and twigs that completely covered the stream. It was a giant dam built by the beavers. It was so

huge that it stretched from one side of the river to the other and almost reached the treetops. It blocked the entire river.

"Wow," said Patsy as she looked up at the size of the whole thing. "I have never seen anything like that, ever. That has to be the biggest dam the beavers have ever built!"

"I think so, too!" replied Rascal, also looking up with an astonished look on his face. "Let's climb this thing and see what is going on. It sounds like all of the noise and laughter is coming from the other side."

CHAPTER 5

WHAT IS THIS HUGE THING?

Rascal, like all raccoons, was naturally very good at climbing. He always enjoyed climbing trees and going as high as he could. Some nights when he was not sleeping over at Buck's tree house, Rascal would go out just before dark and for the pure fun of it, climb one of the tallest trees he could find. Sometimes he would sleep up there for the whole night—it was his natural way.

Now, for Patsy, climbing the huge pile of sticks and logs created a bit of a problem. Being a porcupine, Patsy knew how to climb trees but porcupines like being on the ground most of the time. The only time she ever climbs trees is to reach the very top where the newest and freshest leaves grow. They are the leaves she loves to eat the most,

No salad dressing needed!

the fresh crisp green ones. Patsy would always say, "It is like eating a salad in the sky!"

As Patsy looked up at the tall pile of branches and logs she turned to Rascal and said, "Rascal, climbing this huge thing is not like climbing up a tree. When I climb up a tree my claws and paws will hold onto the tree bark so that I can climb straight up but these trees are lying down and going every which way. I think it would be better

if I just worked my way through the woods to get around this big thing. It will take me longer, but I think it would be safer for me."

"I agree," replied Rascal. "I'll just find you later. Thanks for all of your help and as Buck always says, be careful!"

Patsy gave a wink to Rascal, turned and slowly lumbered off with her long porcupine needles swaying back and forth as she walked away.

Beavers build dams because that is what they are supposed to do. It is their natural way. They will usually pick a small river or a little stream of water gently flowing through the woods and build a dam to block it. It is never an easy project but beavers are masters at it. With their sharp front teeth they will cut down trees along a river bank and drop them with the precision of an expert lumberjack. They will then trim all the branches off of the tree and then drag the branches and the tree down to the river. With a precision that even building engineers can't figure out, they will construct a dam across that stream so tight, so strong, and so compact that only a trickle of water can get through. As the water of the stream backs up against the beaver dam it forms a small lake, or what is called a beaver pond. There the beavers will live, swim around, raise their young, and slap their tails. It is their natural way.

So, as Rascal climbed up this giant wall of tangled branches and logs he realized it was the biggest thing he had ever climbed and was astonished that anyone could ever build such a thing.

As he reached the top and looked over the edge he couldn't believe what he saw!

Surfs up dude!

CHAPTER 6

WHAT FUN!

In front of him was a giant lake. All of the water in the river had backed up to form the biggest pond of water that Rascal had ever seen. It was absolutely huge and it was full of animals, and all of the animals were playing and having a great time. The ducks were jumping off of diving boards, splashing around, and playing in the water. They were having a contest about who could make the biggest splash. The otters had made mud slides along the edge of the lake and were sliding down into the water. Some had even made surfboards and werc sliding. There were rope swings and diving platforms. It was like a giant animal water amusement park and everyone was having a great time. The

YAH-HO!

Cannon Ball!

beavers had even built a big wooden lifeguard station and kept watch in case there was an accident.

"Wow!" said Rascal as he saw the beaver-made lake. "Now I know where all the laughter and noise was coming from and why." So, without any hesitation, Rascal jumped right in. Even raccoons like to swim. It felt great and quickly he got caught up in the fun and

excitement of it all. He swung on the rope swing, jumped from the diving platform, and made one of the biggest splashes of the day. It was fun. The frogs were croaking, the geese were honking, and it looked like everyone was having a great time except the fish. The fish didn't seem to like it all! They didn't like all the noise and disturbance and all the splashing and fooling around. It wasn't normal for river fish. The river was blocked and they couldn't get home. They couldn't swim back and forth. They

Why is he always in such a hurry?

couldn't even find a quiet place to sleep and they didn't like swimming around in a circle all day. The Salmon fish were the most upset of all the fish. This was their river and they loved to race up and down it. Now it was blocked and they didn't like it all. They just swam in a circle—like being in a giant fish bowl.

"Hmm," said Rascal to himself, "there is a lot going on here and I don't think I understand it all. I think I better get out of the water, head home, and tell Buck what I found out." So Rascal climbed out of the water, shook himself off and headed through the woods back to Buck's house. He passed Porcupine Patsy in the woods. She was still slowly lumbering along. Rascal said, "Patsy, when you get there, you won't believe it. Go for a swim, you will love it!"

"Huh?" responded Patsy with a confused look on her face.

"That's alright," said Rascal. "You will understand…if you ever get there! I am off to Buck's house. I am in a hurry and have to go. See you later and thanks for the morning visit. Bye!" Off ran Rascal.

CHAPTER 7

RASCAL TELLS ALL

Rascal took the shortest possible trail, ran most of the way back to Buck's, and was totally out of breath when he reached the tree house. He went up the ladder and ran straight into the kitchen where Buck was making lunch. "Buck, you wouldn't believe it. It is so big, the biggest I have ever seen, it is—it's—" blurted out Rascal, while trying to catch his breath.

"Whoa, slow down, Rascal. Catch your breath. I can tell you are excited. Just give it to me slow and easy. Here, let's have some lunch while you tell me what you found out." Buck put a bowl of nuts and raisins in front of Rascal and poured a little milk over them. Buck knew that was one of Rascal's favorite meals. Rascal then began to tell Buck about everything he saw and heard.

"You said a beaver dam as tall as the trees has created a huge lake in the middle of the woods and the stream is drying up?" Buck asked in almost disbelief. "I think I better go see what is going on. Let's finish our lunch and go visit Bemus Beaver, the biggest and oldest of the beaver clan. He will know what is going on. You said the fish aren't very happy?" asked Buck. "I can see why swimming around in a circle all day is no fun for a stream fish. I would think the Salmon are very upset because they can't finish their yearly marathon run."

"Yup," said Rascal, as he took his last spoonful of raisins and nuts.

Buck put on his hiking boots,

grabbed his hiking stick and said, "I think I will bring a flashlight and a compass just in case we get turned around on our walk back through the woods. It is a long hike to the lower section of the forest and it might be getting dark as we head for home." Rascal nodded his head in agreement, and down the ladder they went and out into the woods.

CHAPTER 8

BUCK GETS INVOLVED

It was a beautiful day—blue sky, white clouds, tall trees, and the smell of moss on the pathway as Buck and Rascal hiked along. "It is just great to be outside," said Buck. "I love to hear the sound the wind makes as it blows through the trees. The whistling sound of pine needles is so different than the chatter and chuckle of leaves.

"Sometimes it sounds like those

leaves are just talking to each other."

Rascal looked up as they walked along and said, "Maybe they are." That put a big smile on Buck's face.

As they walked through the quiet part of the woods, in the direction of the giant beaver dam, Buck began to hear the noise of laughter and yelling that Rascal had described earlier. "We are getting closer," said Rascal. "Hear all that?"

"I sure do!" responded Buck. "It sounds like they are having a good time. Listen to those ducks and geese. They sure are squawking away. I hear beaver tails flapping and even the frogs are croaking!" As Buck and Rascal reached the edge of the big beaver lake, Buck said, "You sure are right, this place looks like a regular water amusement park! Please do me a favor and see if you can find Bemus Beaver and tell him I would like to talk with him."

"Sure thing," said Rascal, and off he went. Buck sat down on a nearby log and just watched. He saw all of the river animals, reptiles, and birds having a great time, but he also saw that the fish didn't like it all. They were swimming in great circles and they didn't look very happy. Most of them were Salmon who had just come upstream and couldn't go any farther. They were bumping into each other, swimming over the top of each other, and looking like they were becoming very angry.

Then, all of a sudden, out of

nowhere, there was a loud crash on the top of the water very close to where Buck was sitting. It sounded as though someone had dropped a big boulder into the water and it made Buck jump up with a startled look. It was Bemus Beaver with a big smile on his face. "Hi Buck. I thought I would swim up quietly

and give you a big tail-slap hello."

"Well," said Buck catching his breath, "you sure did Bemus! You scared the 'ebee-jeebers' out of me!"

"Sorry Buck, I was just fooling around. It is good to see you, though. What's up? Rascal said you were looking for me."

CHAPTER 9

BIGGER IS BETTER

"Yes, Bemus, I am looking for you," responded Buck. "Mind if I ask you what this is all about? Why the giant Beaver Dam? Why the giant lake?"

"Easy to explain," answered Bemus Beaver, as he pulled himself out of the water and came up close to sit next to Buck. "Mind if I chew on a couple branches and crisp leaves while we talk?"

"Go right ahead," said Buck. "Here, let me reach up and snap a few branches off for you."

"Thanks Buck," responded Bemus. "And to answer your question, it is fairly easy. We just thought that bigger was better! We always build our dams on small feeder streams, or what people call little creeks, that flow off of the big river. We cut the logs and branches, build our dams, pack the holes with mud and have our little ponds to raise our young and live happily ever after. Well, this year we got the idea that bigger was better, so let's go big! Let's build the biggest dam we can on the biggest river we can find. So we did! We picked the main river through the woods, got all the beavers in the area to help, worked sun up to sun down and did it! Look at that! Isn't it just beautiful? It is the biggest dam we have ever built and that is the biggest lake any of us have ever seen. And, look at all my animal friends, they are having a ball."

"Hmm," said Buck, "you are right about that. It is the biggest dam I've ever seen, and that is the biggest lake this woods has ever seen, and just about everybody looks like they are having a great time. You did a great job, Bemus. I commend you and the other beavers on your hard work, perseverance, and completion, but as I said, not everybody is having a great time."

"What do you mean Buck? Who

is not enjoying this great big water amusement park?" responded Bemus, looking up at Buck with a surprised look on his face.

"For one," answered Buck, "the fish do not like it at all! Look at them swimming in a big circle, just like they are in a giant fish bowl. They don't have anywhere to go. Those are river fish and they swim up and down the river visiting each other and going on long trips. Look at those Salmon, they are really upset. They can not get up the stream to complete their annual run. All year they go in training, eat right, strengthen up, and get ready for their annual run up the river. Who will be the first this year, who is second, who is third? How far can they actually run before they stop? The dam is blocking them and they can't finish their race. You know the winners lay the eggs that become next year's new Salmon and on it goes, just like it has been almost forever."

CHAPTER 10

WE MEANT NO HARM

"Oh Buck," replied Bemus, "I never thought about that. We meant no harm. We just wanted to try something new and see if we could do it. We would never fool with 'Mother Nature' and be the cause of changing the natural cycle of things."

"You should also see what it looks like downstream," said Buck looking Bemus straight in the eye. "Rascal tells me the stream bed is drying up, the mud is cracking, the trees are wilting, the flowers are gone and most of the stream critters have left. It is not a pretty sight!"

"Okay Buck, maybe 'Bigger' wasn't 'Better' so let's get this problem straightened out. You see things a lot clearer than we do, so what do you suggest?"

"I have an idea," answered Buck, "that just might make everyone happy! How

CLICK!

about if you break down one side of the dam and let the river run through it so that the fish could swim on by? Actually, you could leave a big log across part of the opening so that the Salmon could jump over it. They love to jump and you could give out prizes to the fish who jumped the highest!"

"Great idea," responded Bemus. "That way we can keep most of our lake and everyone can have fun with it and the fish can still swim on by. We'll get right on it. See you later, Buck! Thanks a lot!" And off went Bemus Beaver with a big splash in the water and a call out to all his beaver friends for help.

Buck waved good-bye and headed back up the trail toward home. It didn't

take long for Rascal to catch up. "Hi,
Buck. I heard everything went okay
and I also heard about your idea. All
the animals are talking about it and
they think your idea is brilliant. You

should see the beavers chomping away at the side of the dam. There are wood chips flying all over the place! And the Salmon, they are all stacked up in rows just ready to go. I am going back soon to watch the run. It should be a lot of fun. The beavers said they were going to build a wooden stand with seats so that we can cheer on our favorites as the race goes by."

"Sounds like a bunch of fun," said Buck. "Maybe I will go too, but right now we better head back to the tree house before it gets too late. The day is movin' on by and I am starting to get a little hungry."

"Me too," said Rascal and off
they went.

CHAPTER 11

THE WATER RUNS AGAIN

It didn't take long, only a few days for the beavers to chew down the corner section of their dam and let the water start running through again. The fish swam by, the Salmon started

running again, and the water flowed back again to all the thirsty trees, plants, and flowers. The frogs hopped back, the geese and ducks flew back, and nature came back to its normal cycle.

The beavers left a big log on one side of the water opening, as Buck had suggested. They built a big viewing platform, and all of the animals came daily to cheer and watch the Salmon jump over the log. It was fun for all. It was nice to have everything in the woods back to normal. It felt easy and natural once again, like all things were connected.

Life in the tree house went back to normal. Buck got up every morning, chopped some wood, fed the birds in the bird feeders, made lunches for his animal friends, and at the end of the day, when time permitted, he would go off fishing to his favorite fishing spots. Buck Wilder just loves to fish. He even dreams about it in his sleep!

CHAPTER 12

EVERYTHING WAS JUST FINE

Everything was going fine for a very long time until one day a few of Buck's friends came to visit him with a big problem that was happening in the woods. The animals couldn't figure it out and they needed Buck's help. For some reason the squirrels had gone nuts! Nuts were flying all over and there weren't enough hard hats for the animals to wear. It was a big dilemma and the animals needed Buck's help.

So, visit Buck Wilder in his next outdoor adventure story and find out what he does to help the squirrels and solve the "nutty problem" in the woods. Until then, keep a smile on your face, look up at the clouds, and pay attention to what is going on around you, particularly outside!!

See you later,

SECRET MESSAGE DECODING PAGE

Hidden in this book is a secret Buck Wilder message. You need to figure it out. Hidden in many of the drawings are letters that, when put together, makc up a statement, a Buck Wilder statement. Your job is to find those letters and always remember the message—it's important.

DO NOT write in this book if it's from the library, your classroom, or borrowed from someone.

If you need help finding the hidden letters turn the page.

18 letters make up 4 words.

The secret letters are hidden on the following pages in this order…

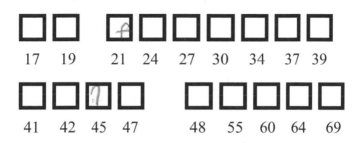

17	19		21	24	27	30	34	37	39

41	42	45	47		48	55	60	64	69

18 letters make up 4 words.

Remember—Don't Write in this Book!

Buck Wilder